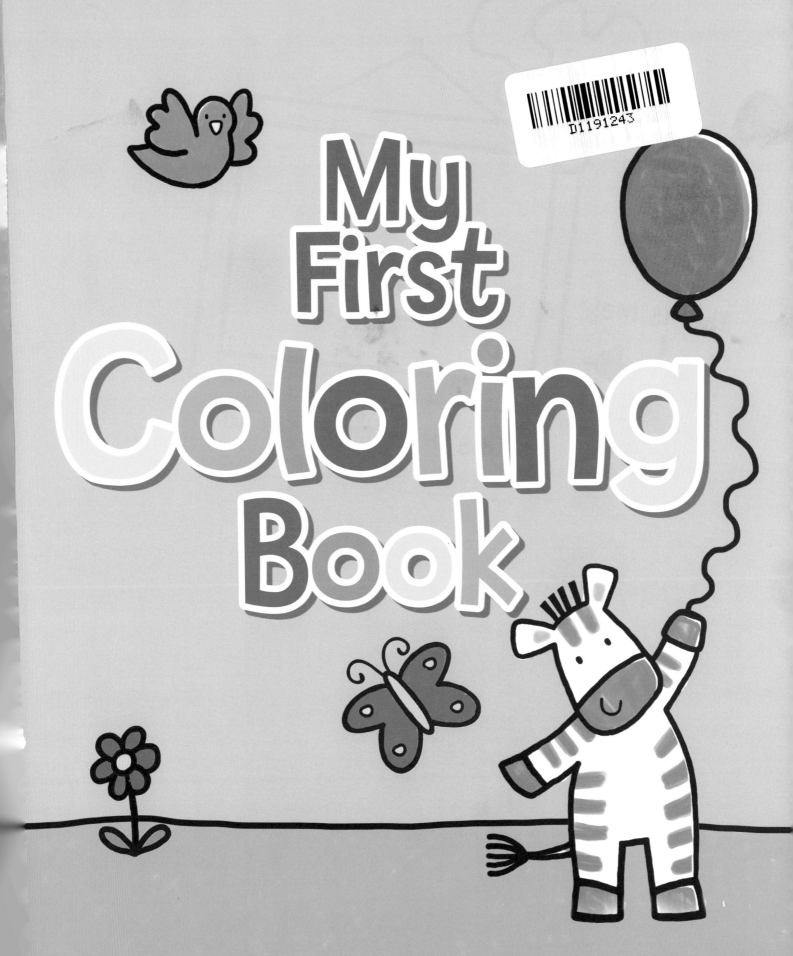

My First Coloring Book

This is me!

This book belongs to

Gwenyth

My First Coloring Book

PaRragon

Color in the train before it steams away! Choo! Choo!

Color the turtles
to make pretty pairs!

Awake

Color in Owl
and Rabbit.

Asleep

color in the caterpillars and some Lunch for them to munch!

Color the clothes on Bear's clothesline.

Can you count three spotted T-shirts?

Color the animals and
their big umbrellas.

Use your
brightest
colors!

Color the happy fish yellow
and the sad fish red.

Happy

Sad

Rabbit has spotted some
Lovely Ladybugs.

finish coloring
the picture.

Color and count four friends on the ferris wheel.

Make this beach towel super cool by finishing the pattern.

Use your brightest colors!

Color the shapes to match the dots to find a juicy fruit!

COLOR in this
handsome piggy!

color in the animals
on the bouncy castle.

Penguin likes to make friends!

Copy the colors to make a friend for Penguin.

Color the animals at the skate park!

Up

Color the birds with bright patterns.

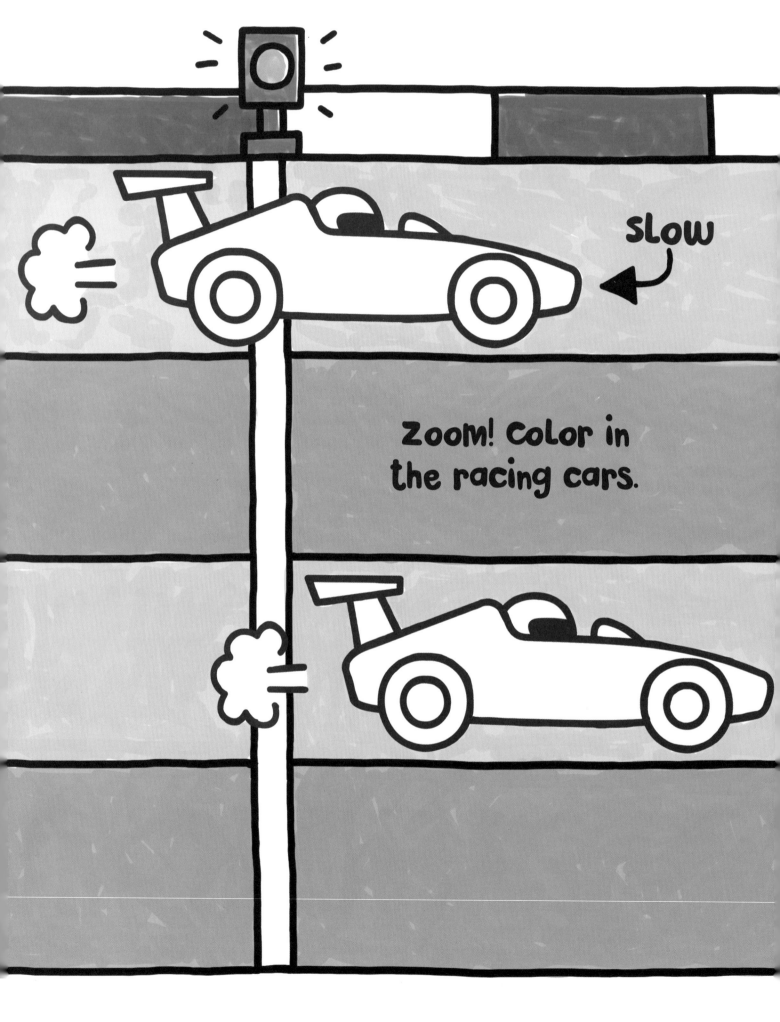

SLOW

ZOOM! Color in the racing cars.

which car is fastest?

fast

Color the patterns on Bear's blanket.

Color the other sides of these pictures to match.

Color the rainbow
using the dots to help you.

count seven colors!

Color in the boat and the passengers.

Land

Sea

Color the rocket before it blasts off into space!

Who's at the door? Draw over the lines, then color the pictures.

Closed

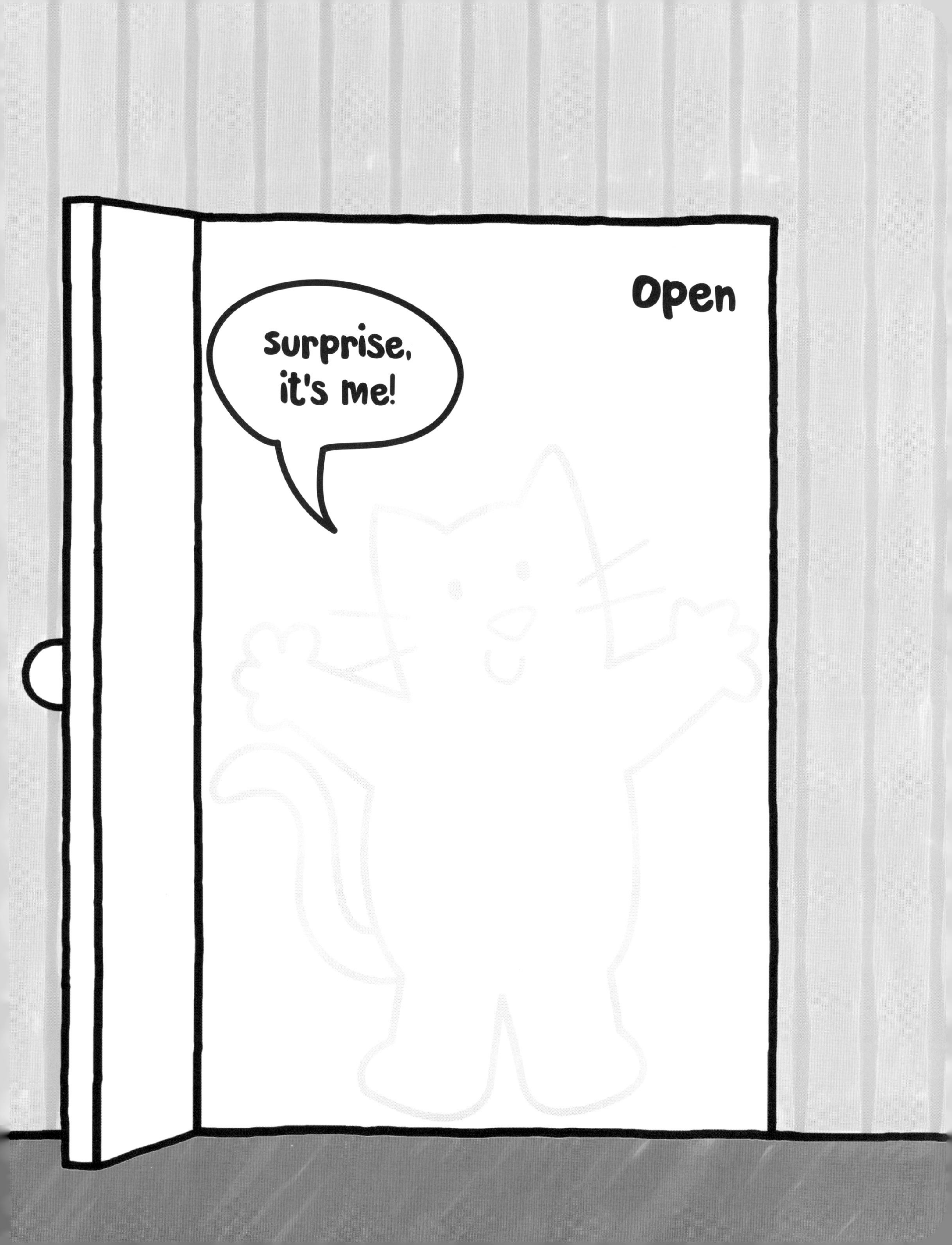
Open
Surprise, it's me!

Color in these shaggy dogs!

Now color and count nine flowers.

Color and count
the spots on
each ladybug.

4

who has the
most spots?

5

6

It's picnic time!
finish coloring
the picture.

Color the planets to make them look out of this world!

Make each kite
a different color.

LOW

High

Spring

Color the
Leaves on this
tree green.

Autumn

Color some brown leaves falling from this tree.

Draw over the lines, then color in your troll picture.

Color the tall flowers red and the short flowers yellow!

short

Tall

which flower is the tallest?

Monkey loves jumping in the mud!

Copy the colors to make
your own Messy Monkey!

Color in King and Queen
Bear and their castle.

Oh, dear! Elephant is too heavy for a seesaw ride with Mouse!

Light

count two butterflies.

finish coloring
the picture.

Color the shapes to match the dots to see something you'd find at sea.

Color in Bear and Rabbit sharing some popcorn.

Color the windows blue and the flags yellow. Then color the rest of the palace!

Can you spot seven flags?

Color more slices of yummy pizza!

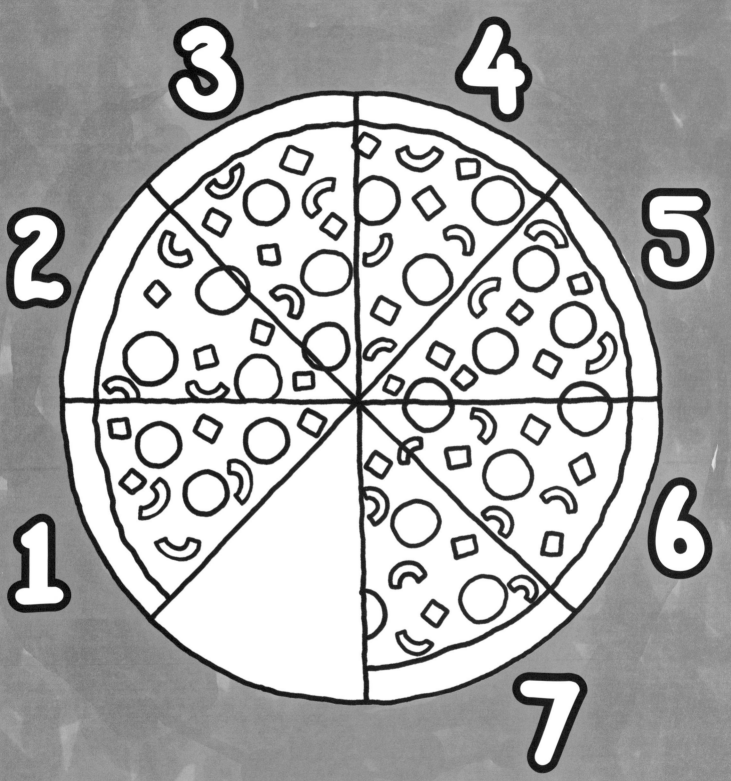

color and count seven slices of pizza.

Captain Tiger is setting sail!

Copy the colors to
match the picture
on the Left!

Color this tablecloth using the dots to help you!

Color all the buttons in Pig's collection.

color these wise owls using the dots to help you.

color six birds
yellow and five
birds red!

Color the shiny coins and jewels
in this treasure chest!

Brighten up this snowman using your favorite colors.

Color in the picture of Mouse and his new house!

Can you count four chimneys?

color in the
handprints!

color these seashells on the seashore.

Add some color to these summer T-shirts.

Color the tall skyscrapers red and the short houses purple.

Color in these fun faces made out of food!

Happy

Sad

Laughing

Sleepy

Count two mouths made from bananas!

zebra is watching TV.
Draw over the Lines, then
color in the picture.

color in the TV picture, too!

count six stars.

It's cat's birthday! Color in the party hats.

Use your brightest colors!

What a lovely
day for a walk!

finish coloring the picture.

Color in the cupcake to make it Look extra tasty!

Now color this one to match.

Color in the pattern on squirrel's tail!

Zoom! Bang! Make the fireworks bright and colorful.

Add some color to brighten up these elephants.

Color the sheep in lots of different colors!

Color the bubbles using the dots to help you.

Color and count the turtles in each tower.

Color the bunnies brown and the pigs pink!

Count four bunnies.

Add some color to these wallpaper patterns.

Color in the things on these shelves.